P9-ECY-145

Text and illustrations copyright © 2009 by Deborah Zemke
All rights reserved
Published in the United States 2009 by
Blue Apple Books, 515 Valley Street, Maplewood, N.J. 07040
www.blueapplebooks.com

Distributed in the U.S. by Chronicle Books
First Edition
Printed in China

ISBN: 978-1-934706-57-2

2 4 6 8 10 9 7 5 3 1

Deborah Zemke

How to Win Friends and Influence Creatures

Blue Apple Books

When everyone else
is talking...

learn to listen.

Don't
open
your
mouth...

just to hear yourself

ROAR!

If you lead...

others

    will

        follow.

Fancy feathers don't make the bird.

Don't dress like a peacock...

if you're a penguin.

Sometimes it's best...

to be LAST in line.

Keep your tentacles
to yourself...

even when
others don't.

Walk softly
      and carry a big banana...

big enough to share.

DON'T...

hog the mudbath.

Stand up straight...

There may only be one leader,

but it takes the whole pack...

Don't invite
anyone over...

just for dessert.

If you're invited for a sleepover...

Don't SNORE.

When you meet someone...

DO NOT
lick your chops
and say:

Croak good things about others.

Try not to repeat yourself. Try not to repeat yourself. Try not

to show others...